THIRST

Amélie Nothomb

THIRST

*Translated from the French
by Alison Anderson*

Europa
editions

Europa Editions
1 Penn Plaza, Suite 6282
New York, N.Y. 10019
www.europaeditions.com
info@europaeditions.com

Copyright © 2019 by Editions Albin Michel, Paris
First publication 2021 by Europa Editions

Translation by Alison Anderson
Original title: *Soif*
Translation copyright © 2021 by Europa Editions

Library of Congress Cataloging in Publication Data is available
ISBN 978-1-60945-660-3

Nothomb, Amélie
Thirst

Book design by Emanuele Ragnisco
www.mekkanografici.com

Cover image by Ginevra Rapisardi

Prepress by Grafica Punto Print – Rome

Printed and bound in Great Britain by Clays Ltd, Elcograf S.p.A.

THIRST

I always knew I would be sentenced to death. The advantage of such knowledge is that I can focus my attention where it is warranted: on the details.

I thought my trial would be a parody of justice. And indeed, it was, but not in the way I expected. I had imagined a hastily expedited formality, but I was given the works. The prosecutor left nothing to chance.

The witnesses for the prosecution paraded past, one after the other. I couldn't believe my eyes when I saw the newlyweds from Cana, the first beneficiaries of my miracle working.

"This man has the power to change water into wine," declared the husband, deadly serious. "And yet, he waited until the end of the wedding to exercise his talent. He enjoyed seeing how anxious and humiliated we were, when he could so easily have prevented it. Because of him, we served the good wine after the inferior one. We were the laughingstock of the village."

I calmly looked my accuser in the eye. He held my gaze, confident in his reasoning.

The royal official stepped up to describe the ill will with which I had cured his son.

"And how is the child doing now?" my lawyer, the most inefficient office clerk you could possibly imagine, could not help but ask.

"He is fine. To his credit! With magic like his, a single word suffices."

All thirty-seven miracle recipients took a turn airing their dirty laundry. I found the once-possessed man of Capernaum to be the most entertaining:

"Since the exorcism, my life has been incredibly boring!"

The erstwhile blind man complained of how ugly the world was, the former leper declared that no one gave him alms anymore, the fishermen's union from Tiberias accused me of having favored one crew over all the others, and Lazarus described how horrible it was to live with the smell of a corpse clinging to his skin.

From the looks of it, it had not been necessary to bribe them or even encourage them. They all came to testify against me of their own free will. Several of them said what a relief it was to be able to vent their frustration in the presence of the culprit at last.

In the presence of the culprit.

I only appear calm to people. It took a supreme effort on my part to listen to all these litanies without reacting. Every time, I looked the witness in the eye with no other expression than gentle astonishment. Every time, they held my gaze with disdain, defying me, looking at me with scorn.

The mother of a child I'd healed went so far as to accuse me of having ruined her life.

"When my little boy was unwell, he was quiet. Now he wiggles and screams and cries, I don't get a moment's peace, and not a wink of sleep at night."

"But did you not ask my client to cure your son?" the office clerk asked.

"To cure him, yes, not to make him as maddening as he was before he got ill."

"Perhaps you should have made that clear."

"Is he omniscient, or isn't he?"

A good question. I always know Τι, and never Πῶς. I know

the direct object but never the adverbial phrase. Therefore, no, I am not omniscient: I discover the adverbs as I go along, and they throw me for a loop. People are right to say the devil is in the details.

In truth, not only did they need no encouragement from the prosecution to testify, they also ardently desired to. Their readiness to speak against me was staggering. All the more in that it was strictly unnecessary. They all knew I would be sentenced to death.

There is nothing mysterious about prophecy. They knew my powers and could see for themselves that I had not used them to save myself. They were in no doubt, therefore, as to the outcome of the matter.

Why were they so eager to inflict such pointless censure upon me? The enigma of evil is nothing in comparison to that of mediocrity. As they were testifying, I could tell how much they were enjoying it. They delighted in behaving wretchedly in front of me. They were simply disappointed that my suffering wasn't more visible. Not that I wanted to deny them that supreme pleasure, but my astonishment far outweighed my indignation.

I am a man, and nothing human is foreign to me. And yet, I cannot understand what came over them as they were ranting and raving such abominations. I consider my incomprehension to be a failure, a sign of neglect.

Pontius Pilate had received his instructions about me, and I could see how put out he was—not that he liked me in any way, but because the witnesses irritated the rational man in him. My stupefaction deceived him; he sought to give me an opportunity to protest against the unending stream of nonsense:

"Defendant, do you have anything to say?" he asked, his expression that of an intelligent being addressing his peer.

"No," I replied.

He nodded, as if to imply it was pointless to throw a line to someone who was that unconcerned by his own fate.

In truth, I said nothing because I had too much to say. Had I spoken, I would not have been able to hide my scorn. Feeling scorn is a torment to me. I have been a man for long enough to know that some feelings cannot be repressed. What matters is letting them go by without trying to counter them: that way they leave no trace.

Scorn is a sleeping devil. A devil that fails to act will soon begin to fade. In the courtroom, words are as good as actions. Keeping my scorn silent was as good as preventing it from acting.

Pilate turned to his counselors:

"The proof that these testimonies are false is that our man has not resorted to magic to set himself free."

"And it is not on those grounds that we call for his conviction."

"I know. I want nothing more than to convict him. The only thing is that I would have preferred not to feel as if I am doing so for fraudulent reasons!"

"In Rome, people require bread and circuses. Here they require bread and miracles."

"So be it. If it's political, then it doesn't bother me anymore."

Pilate stood up and declared, "Defendant, you shall be crucified."

I appreciated his frugal language. The genius of Latin is that it never uses more words than are necessary. I would have hated it if he had said, "You shall be crucified to death." When it comes to crucifixion there is no other outcome.

The fact remains that, coming from his lips, it had the desired effect. I looked at the witnesses, and I could sense how embarrassed they felt, albeit too late. And yet, they had all known I would be convicted, and they had gone so far as to actively contribute to my sentence. Now they were pretending to find that sentence excessive and to be shocked by the barbarity of the procedure. Some of them even tried to catch my gaze in order to dissociate themselves from what would ensue. I looked away.

I did not know that I would die like this. It was not an easy thing to accept. I thought about the pain, for a start. My mind shied away: it is impossible to comprehend such suffering.

Crucifixion is reserved for the most heinous crimes. I did not expect such humiliation. But that is what they had asked of Pilate. It was pointless wasting my time in conjectures: Pilate had not objected. He had to condemn me to death, but he could have opted for beheading, for example. At what point did I rub him the wrong way? Probably when I would not disown my miracle working.

I could not lie: those miracles truly were my handiwork. And contrary to what the witnesses had attested, those miracles required an unbelievable effort on my part. No one had ever taught me the art of accomplishing them.

And then I had a strange thought: at least this torture that awaited me would not require any miracles on my part. All I had to do was let myself go.

"Will he be crucified today?" someone asked.

Pilate considered the question and looked at me. He must have seen that something was missing, because he replied:

"No. Tomorrow."

When I was once again alone in my cell, I knew what he wanted me to feel: fear.

Pilate was right. Until that night, I had never really known what fear was. In the Garden of Gethsemane, the night before my arrest, it was sorrow and dereliction that had caused my tears.

Now, I was discovering fear. Not the fear of death, that most common of abstract notions, but the fear of crucifixion: a very concrete fear.

I have the unerring conviction that I am the most incarnate of human beings. When I lie down to go to sleep, the mere abandonment of it procures such pleasure that I have to stop myself from moaning. Eating the humblest gruel, drinking even standing water would cause me to sigh with delight if I did not keep myself strictly in line. More than once, I have wept with bliss on breathing in the morning air.

And the opposite is also true: the most benign toothache can cause abnormal torment. I recall cursing my fate over a splinter. I hide this sensitive nature as carefully as the previous one: it does not tally with what I am supposed to represent. Yet another misunderstanding.

In my thirty-three years here on earth, I have had time to notice it: my father's greatest success has been incarnation. That a disincarnate power could come up with the idea of inventing the body remains a masterful stroke of genius. Is it any surprise the creator was overwhelmed by his creation, the impact of which he could not foresee?

I'd like to say that this is why he created me, but it would not be true.

It would have been a good reason.

Humans complain, rightfully, of the imperfections of the body. The explanation is obvious: what would a house be worth if it were designed by a homeless architect? We only excel at things we practice daily. My father never had a body. For an ignorant sort, I think he did a remarkably good job.

My fear that night was a physical dizziness at the thought of what I would have to go through. Those who are tortured are expected to rise to the occasion. When they do not scream with pain, we say how brave they are. I suspect it is something else: I will find out what it is.

I feared the nails through my hands and feet. That was stupid: there would surely be greater pain. But that one I could imagine at least.

The jailer said to me:

"Try to get some sleep. You need to be in good shape tomorrow."

On seeing my ironic expression, he added:

"Don't laugh. It takes good health to die. Don't say I didn't warn you."

And that is true. In addition, this was my last opportunity to sleep, and I do so like sleep. I did try, I lay down on the floor, I surrendered my body to rest: it wanted nothing to do with me. Whenever I closed my eyes, instead of finding sleep, I came upon terrifying images.

And so, I did what everyone does: to fight off the unbearable thoughts, I turned to other ones.

I relived my first miracle, my favorite. I realized, to my relief, that the newlyweds' appalling testimony had not tarnished this memory.

It had not, however, gotten off to a very good start. Going to a wedding with one's mother is a trying experience. My mother may well be pure of soul, but she nevertheless remains a normal woman. She kept looking at me out of the corner of her eye as if to say, well, my son, what are you waiting for to find yourself a bride? I pretended not to notice.

I must confess I do not much like weddings. I cannot really work out why. It's the sort of sacrament that fills me with anxiety, something I understand all the less in that it does not concern me. I will not be getting married and do not regret it.

It was an ordinary wedding: a celebration where people displayed more joy than they really felt. I knew they were expecting something more from me. What could it be? I had no idea.

A distinguished meal: bread and grilled fish, wine. The wine was not great, but the bread came warm from the oven, with a lovely crust, and the fish was salted to perfection and filled me with delight. I concentrated on my food so I could enjoy all of the flavor and texture. My mother seemed embarrassed that I was not talking with the other guests. In this respect, I resemble her: she's not very talkative. Making small talk is something I cannot do, and neither can she.

My feelings for the bride and groom were those of amiable indifference, of the sort one feels for the friends of one's parents. It must have been the third time I had met them, and, as always, they exaggerated, "We knew Jesus when he was a little boy," and, "You look different with a beard." The excessive familiarity of humans makes me feel slightly ill at ease. I wish I had never seen those newlyweds. Our relationship would have been more authentic.

I missed Joseph. That good man, who was hardly more talkative than my mother or me, excelled at playing the part: he listened so carefully that you thought you could hear his reply. I did not inherit that virtue. When people are making small talk, I don't even pretend to listen.

"What are you thinking about?" my mother murmured.

"Joseph."

"Why do you call him that?"

"You know why."

I was never sure she really did know why, but if you have to explain that sort of thing to your mother, you'll never see the end of it.

There was a sudden commotion.

"They're out of wine," said my mother.

I couldn't see the problem. No more of that plonk, and so what! Cool water was better at quenching one's thirst, so I went on eating conscientiously. It took me a moment to grasp that, to this family, a lack of wine was a source of irredeemable dishonor.

"They are out of wine," my mother said again, pointedly.

An abyss opened at my feet. What a strange woman my mother is! She wants me to be normal, but at the same time I'm meant to work miracles!

How alone I felt at that moment. But I couldn't put it off any longer. Then I had a flash of intuition. I said:

"Fetch two pitchers of water."

The master of the house gave orders, I must be obeyed, and a great silence fell over the gathering. If I stopped to think, all would be lost. What was required was the opposite of thought. I obliterated myself. I knew that just beneath my skin there lay power, and that to get there, thought must be abolished. I yielded the floor to what, from that moment on, I would refer to as the husk, and I do not know what happened. For an insurmountable lapse of time, I ceased to exist.

When I came to, the guests were ecstatic:

"This is the best wine we've ever drunk in all the land!"

Everyone was tasting the new wine; their faces wore the sort of expression expected of them during religious ceremonies. I repressed a colossal desire to burst out laughing.

And so, my father had deemed it fit for me to discover this power during a shortage of wine. What a sense of humor! And how could anyone disapprove? What could be more important than wine? I had been a man long enough to know that joy is not a given, and that very good wine is often the only way to find it.

The wedding was flowing with good cheer. The newly-weds looked happy at last. The urge to dance came over them, and the spirit of the wine left no one untouched.

"One must not serve the best wine after the inferior one!" people remarked to their hosts.

I can attest that it was not said in a critical way. Moreover, this assertion is quite open to debate. I believe the contrary. It is better to begin with an ordinary wine in order to instill joy in people's hearts. For it is when people are as joyful as they can be that they are capable of welcoming a great wine and giving it the supreme attention it deserves.

That is my favorite miracle. It was not hard to choose—it's the only miracle I like. I had just discovered the husk, and I was dazzled. The first time you do something that is so far beyond you, you immediately forget the disproportionate effort it took, and remember only the wonder of the result.

And besides, the issue was wine at a feast. Later on, things took a turn for the worse—at stake were matters of suffering, illness, death, or catching poor fish I would have rather left alive and free. Above all, knowingly resorting to the power of the husk has turned out to be a thousand times harder than its discovery.

The worst thing is people's expectations. No one in Cana, apart from my mother, required anything of me. Later, wherever I went, they had seen me coming, they'd left a leper or an invalid in my path. When I accomplished a miracle, it was no longer a gift of grace, but the fulfillment of my duty.

How many times did I read in the gaze of a dying person or someone holding out his stump to me, not an entreaty, but a threat! If they had dared to formulate their thought, it would have been, "You've become famous with your nonsense, now you'd better take responsibility for it, otherwise, just you wait and see!" There were times when I did not accomplish the miracle they'd asked for because I didn't have the strength to obliterate myself and release the power of the husk: how they hated me for it!

Later on, I gave it some thought, and I did not approve of my wondrous feats. They gave the wrong impression, this was not what I had to come to deliver; love was no longer free, it had to serve a purpose. Not to mention what I discovered this morning, during the trial: none of those who had benefited from my miracles felt the slightest gratitude. On the contrary, they reproached me bitterly for those miracles, even the bride and groom from Cana.

I don't want to remember any of that. All I want to remember is the joy at Cana, the innocence of our happiness, drinking that wine that had come out of nowhere, the purity of our initial intoxication. Such intoxication is only worth it if it's shared. That evening at Cana, we were all drunk and in the best way. Yes, my mother was tipsy, and it suited her. Since Joseph's death, I had rarely seen her look happy. My mother was dancing, I danced with her, my dear old mama I love so well. My drunkenness told her that I loved her, and I could sense her response, even though she said nothing, my son, I know there is something special about you, I suspect someday it will it pose a problem, but for the time being I'm just proud of you and happy to be drinking this good wine you made for us with your magic.

And that night, I truly was drunk, and my drunkenness was holy. Before the incarnation, I did not weigh anything. The paradox is that in order to experience lightness you must weigh something. Inebriation frees you from weight and gives you the impression you are about to take flight. Our spirit does not fly, it moves unhindered, and that's very different. Birds have a body; their flight is nothing less than conquest. I can never repeat it often enough: having a body is the best thing there is.

I expect that I will think just the opposite tomorrow, when my body is being tortured. And yet, for all that, can I disown the discoveries it has given me? The greatest joys of my life are those I have known through my body. And must I point out that my soul and spirit played an important part as well?

The miracles, too, I obtained through my body. What I call the husk is physical. To have access to it presupposes the temporary obliteration of the spirit. I have never been any other man than myself, but I am deeply convinced that every one of us has this power. The reason it is so rarely put to use is that it's very difficult to access. One must have the strength and the courage to elude the spirit, and that is not a metaphor. A few human beings managed to do this before me, and a few human beings will manage after me.

My knowledge of time does not differ from my knowledge of my fate: I know Τι, but I know nothing of Πώς. Names belong to Πώς, and so I don't know the name of a writer in the future who will say, "The most profound thing in man is his skin." He will come close to a revelation, but in any case, even those who glorify him will not understand the concrete nature of his words.

It's not exactly the skin, it's just beneath. Therein lies omnipotence.

Tonight, there will be no miracle. There is no way I can shy away from what awaits me tomorrow. Not that I wouldn't like to.

Just once, I misused the power of the husk. I was hungry, and the fruit on the fig tree was not ripe. My desire to bite into a fig—warm with sunshine, juicy and sweet—was so great that I cursed the tree, and condemned it to never again bear fruit. I said it was for a parable, not the most convincing.

How could I have been so unfair? It was not fig season. That was my only destructive miracle. In truth, on that day, I was ordinary. Frustrated by my greedy appetite, I allowed desire to turn to anger. And yet, appetite can be a very fine thing, provided it is kept intact. I needed only remind myself that in a month or two I would be able to satisfy it.

I am not without faults. There is an anger inside me that would like nothing better than to explode. There was the episode with the merchants at the Temple: at least my cause was a just one. From there to saying, "I came not to send peace, but a sword," there's still some leeway.

On the eve of my death, I have realized I am ashamed of nothing, except the fig tree. I really did take it out on an innocent creation. No point in moping in pointless regret, it simply bothers me that I cannot go and sit quietly next to the tree, embrace it, and ask its forgiveness. All it would have to do is forgive me, and its curse would end there and then, it would bear fruit once again, and be proud of the delicious weight on its branches.

I recall the orchard I walked through with the disciples. The apple trees were collapsing with the weight of the fruit, we gorged ourselves on those apples, the best we'd ever tasted—fragrant, crisp, and juicy. We stopped when we could eat no more, our bellies about to explode, and we fell to the ground, laughing at our gluttony.

"Look at all these apples we won't be able to eat, that no one will eat!" said John. "It's so sad!"

"Sad for who?" I asked.

"The trees."

"Do you think so? Apple trees are happy to produce their apples, even if no one eats them."

"How do you know?"

"Try being an apple tree."

John was silent for a moment, and then he said:

"You're right."

"We're the ones who feel sad—at the thought we can't eat all the apples."

Everyone burst out laughing.

I was a better man with the apple tree than with the fig tree. Why was that? Because I had satisfied my appetite. We are better people when we have had our pleasure, it's as simple as that.

Alone in my cell, I feel as if I am that fig tree I cursed. It makes me sad, and so I do what everyone does: I try to move on to something else. The problem with this method is that it doesn't work very well. Apple tree, fig tree—I wondered which tree Judas used to hang himself. They told me the branch broke. The tree must not have been very strong, because Judas didn't weigh very much.

I always knew Judas would betray me. But, in keeping with the nature of my prescience, I didn't know how he would go about it.

Our first encounter was particularly striking. I was in a vil-lage in the middle of nowhere where I understood no one. The longer I spoke, the more I could sense their hostility increasing, so much so that I began to see myself through their eyes, and I shared their consternation regarding this clown who had come to preach love to them.

In the crowd, there was this dark, skinny young man who oozed malaise from every pore. This is how he questioned me:

"You say we must love our neighbor—do you love me?"

"Of course."

"That makes no sense. No one loves me. Why would you love me?"

"I don't need a reason to love you."

"Yeah, really. What a load of hogwash."

People laughed in complicity with the young man. He seemed touched: this was visibly the first time he had gar-nered approval in his village.

And then I had the revelation of what was to come: this man would betray me, and my heart fell.

The gathering broke up. He alone still stood there before me.

"Would you like to join us?" I asked him.

"Who do you mean, us?"

I pointed to the disciples sitting on rocks off to one side.

"These are my friends," I said.

"And who am I?"

"You're my friend."

"What makes you so sure?"

I realized that to answer would serve no purpose. There was something off about him.

I suppose we all have a friend like that: other people don't understand the connection. The disciples had all taken to each other right from the start. But, for Judas, nothing seemed straightforward.

And he didn't make things any easier. Whenever he felt that he was liked, he went and said the very thing it took to elicit rejection:

"Leave me alone, I've got nothing to do with you!"

This would be followed by endless discussions, where his ill will became patently clear.

"What makes you think you're so different from us, Judas?"

"I wasn't born with a silver spoon in my mouth."

"And neither were most of us."

"It's just plain obvious I'm not like you, isn't it?"

"What do you mean, like us? Simon and John, for example, have nothing in common."

"Yes, they do: in Jesus's presence they stand there gaping."

"They don't stand there gaping. They love and admire him, like we do."

"I don't. I like him, but I don't admire him."

"Then why are you following him?"

"Because he asked me to."

"You didn't have to."

"I've seen plenty of other prophets who are just as good."

"He's not a prophet."

"Prophet, Messiah, it's all the same."

"Not at all. He is bringing love."

"What is this love of his?"

With Judas, you always had to start from scratch. He was enough to discourage anybody, he discouraged me more than once. Loving him was nothing less than a challenge, and I loved him all the more for it. Not that I prefer difficult love, on the contrary, but because, with him, the additional effort was crucial.

If I had only spent time with the other disciples, I might have forgotten that it was for people like Judas that I had come: living problems, troublemakers, the ones Simon refers to as bloody pains in the neck.

"What is this love of his?" A good question. Night and day, you have to search within for this love. When you find it, it is so powerfully obvious, that you no longer understand why you found it so difficult to unearth it. But then you must stay in its never-ending flow. Love is energy and, therefore, movement. Nothing stagnates in it, the point is to throw yourself into its current without pausing to wonder how you will manage to hold on. It is not proof against plausibility.

When you're in it, you see it. It's not a metaphor: how many times have I been granted the possibility to see the ray of light that connects two human beings who love one another? When it is addressed to you, this light becomes less visible but more sensitive, you perceive its rays as they enter your skin—and there is no better feeling. If it were possible to hear it, you would make out the crackling of sparks.

Thomas only believes what he sees. Judas did not even believe what he saw. He said, "I don't want to be misled by my senses." When a platitude is heard for the first time, it causes a bit of a stir.

Judas is one of those figures who will generate the greatest amount of commentary in history. Is that any surprise, given the part he had to play? People will assert that he was the prototype of the traitor; such theories die hard. The amount of hot air created by this condemnation will lead, obviously, to its opposite. On the basis of an identical dearth of infor- mation, Judas will be proclaimed the most loving of disciples, the purest, the most innocent. The judgment of mankind is so predictable that I admire everyone for taking themselves so seriously.

Judas was a strange fellow. Something about him was impervious to any form of analysis. There was very little about him that was incarnate. To be more precise, he perceived only negative sensations. He would say, "I have a backache," as if he had discovered a theorem.

If I said to him, "What a pleasant spring breeze," he would reply, "Anyone could say that."

"True enough, which makes it all the more delightful," I insisted.

He would shrug, not wanting to waste his time replying to a simpleton.

In the beginning, all the disciples had trouble with him. Due to their kindness, they tried to comfort him. This made Judas very aggressive. Gradually, they realized it would be better not to talk to him too often. But also, not to ignore him: he was so touchy that he feared silence more than words.

Judas was an ongoing problem, primarily for himself. When there was no reason to get angry, he got angry. When there were only annoyances, he lost his temper. Consequently, it was preferable to be with him in moments of adversity; he fit in better. Until I met Judas, I didn't know there were people that were perpetually offended. I don't know if he was the first, but I do know he wasn't the last.

We loved him. He realized this and tried to prove us wrong.

"I'm no angel, I have a foul character."

"We've noticed," one of us replied, with a smile.

"What? You're a fine one to talk!"

When he wasn't conducting his own imaginary trial, he labored at unraveling our affection.

He hated lying. When I brought the subject up, I noticed he could not really say what it was. For example, he was unable to differentiate between lies and secrets.

"Withholding some true information is not the same as lying," I said to him.

"The moment you don't tell the whole truth you are lying," he replied.

He was like a dog with a bone. As I was getting nowhere with theory, I tried sophistry.

"A new law has decreed that hunchbacks will be sentenced to death. Your neighbor is afflicted with a hump, and the authorities ask you if you know any hunchbacks. You say no, of course. This is not a lie."

"Yes, it is."

"No, it's a secret."

If Judas had been more present in his own body, he would have possessed what he was lacking: subtlety. The body grasps what the mind fails to understand.

I have few memories of the time before incarnation. Things literally eluded me: what can you retain from things you can't feel? There is no greater art than that of living. The best artists are those whose senses possess the greatest finesse. It is pointless to leave a trace elsewhere than in one's own skin.

If one would just listen to it, one would realize that the body is always intelligent. In some distant future, it will be possible to measure people's intellectual quotient. It will serve no purpose. Fortunately, it will never be possible to evaluate an individual's degree of incarnation other than through intuition: their supreme value.

A source of trouble in all this will be people who are capable of leaving their body. If they only knew how easy it is, they wouldn't have so much admiration for this prowess of theirs—at best useless, at worst, dangerous.

If a noble spirit leaves their body, it causes no harm. No doubt a journey can be found pleasant for the sole reason that it has not yet been taken. Similarly, walking down the street in the opposite direction from one's usual daily route can be entertaining. Period. The problem is that mediocre minds will try to imitate this experience. My father would have done better to put incarnation under lock and key. Obviously, I can understand his concern for human freedom.

But the result of the separation between a weak mind and its body will prove disastrous for that individual and for others.

An incarnate being never commits abominable acts. If he kills, it is in self-defense. He does not get carried away without a just cause. Evil always has its origin in the mind. Without the safeguard of the body, spiritual damage can begin.

At the same time, I understand. I too am afraid of suffering. We seek to become disincarnate in order to ensure ourselves of an emergency exit. Tomorrow, I won't have one.

This night I am writing from does not exist. The Gospels are categorical: my last night of freedom is set in the Garden of Gethsemane. The following morning, I am sentenced with immediate effect. I actually see this as a form of humanity: to make someone wait increases their torture.

And yet, there is this unexplored dimension that I don't think I've made up: a time belonging to another order that I've inserted between myself and death. I'm like everyone, I'm afraid to die. I don't think I will be given special treatment.

Did I choose? Apparently. How could I have chosen to be me? For the reason that governs the vast majority of choices: unconsciously. If we knew what we were doing, we would not choose to live.

Nevertheless, I made the worst choice. Which must mean that I was as unconscious as can be. At least when it comes to love, things don't happen this way. That's how you know you're in love: because you haven't chosen to be. People with big egos don't fall in love, because they can't stand not being able to choose. They are attracted to the people they pick: that's not love.

In that inconceivable moment when I chose my fate, I did not know that it would mean falling in love with Mary Magdalene. Actually, I think I will call her Madeleine: I don't like double names, and I find it tedious to call her the Magdalene. As for calling her Mary, that's out of the question. It's never a good idea to confuse your sweetheart with your mother.

There is no such thing as causality in love, because we don't choose. We invent the notion of "because" afterwards for our own pleasure. I fell in love with Madeleine the moment I saw her. I could quibble: if it was my sense of sight that held the role of making me fall in love, one could attribute the cause to Madeleine's extreme beauty. The fact is, she was silent, and so I saw her before I heard her. Madeleine's voice is even more beautiful than her looks: had I come to know her through my hearing, the result would have been exactly the same. If I were to continue along this train of thought with my three other senses, my intentions would begin to verge on the shameless.

It's not surprising that I fell in love with Madeleine. The fact she fell in love with me, on the other hand, is far more extraordinary. However, that is exactly what happened the moment she saw me.

We told each other the story a thousand times, knowing all the while that this fiction was getting carried away. It was a good thing we did: it gave us boundless pleasure.

"When I saw your face, I could not get over it. I didn't know that so much beauty was possible. And then you looked at me, and it made things worse: I didn't know anyone could look at me like that. When you look at me, I have trouble breathing. Do you look at everybody like that?"

"I don't think so. I'm not known for it. And you're a fine one to talk. Your gaze is famous, Jesus. People travel for miles to have you gaze at them."

"I don't gaze at anyone the way I gaze at you."

"I should hope not."

Love concentrates certainty and doubt: you are as sure of

being loved as of doubting that love, not alternately, but with disconcerting simultaneity. If you try to get rid of your doubting side by asking your beloved a thousand questions, you end up denying the radically ambiguous nature of love.

Madeleine had known many men, and I had known no women. Nevertheless, our lack of experience made us equal. Confronted with what was happening to us, our ignorance was that of a newborn infant. The trick is in embracing this convulsive state with enthusiasm. I daresay I'm exceedingly good at it, and Madeleine is too. Her case is all the more admirable in that men have accustomed her to expect the worst, and yet she has not become mistrustful. To her credit.

How I miss her! I summon her in my thoughts, but it's no substitute. Maybe it would be more dignified if I refused to let her see me like this. Still, I would give anything to see her again and hold her in my arms.

They say that love is blind. I have found it's the opposite. Universal love is an act of generosity that presupposes painful clarity. As for the state of being in love, it makes us see splendors that are invisible to the naked eye.

Madeleine's beauty was well known. However, no one knows better than I do just how beautiful she is. It takes courage to be able to stomach that much beauty.

I often asked her, and there was nothing rhetorical about it, "What's it like being so beautiful?"

She tended to dodge the issue:

"It depends on who with."

Or:

"It's all right."

Or even:

"What a nice thing to say."

The last time I insisted:

"I'm not trying to be gallant. It really does interest me."

She sighed.

"Until I met you, on the rare occasion when I was aware of it, I would feel nailed to the wall. Now that it's you looking at me, I have learned to be glad of it."

Among the things I did not tell her, for the very reason that it would confuse matters, there was this: of all the joys I had known with her, none could compare with the contemplation of her beauty.

"Stop looking at me like that," she would say every so often.

"You are my glass of water."

There is no greater pleasure than a glass of water when you are dying of thirst.

The only Evangelist who has shown talent as a writer worthy of the name is John. That is also why his words are the least reliable. "Whosoever drinketh of the water that I shall give him shall never thirst": I never said it, it would have been a misrepresentation.

It's no coincidence that I chose this part of the world: it was not enough for me that this is a place of political upheaval. I needed a land of great thirst. No other sensation more eloquently evokes what I seek to inspire than thirst. That is surely why no one has experienced it as often as I have.

Truth to tell: what you feel when you are dying of thirst is something you must cultivate. Therein lies the mystical urge. It is not its metaphor. When you are no longer hungry, that is called satiety. When you are no longer tired, that is called rest. When you cease to suffer, that is called comfort. When you are no longer thirsty, there is no word for it.

Language, in its wisdom, has understood that there must be no antonym for thirst. You can quench thirst, yet the noun for it does not exist.

There are people who do not consider themselves mystics.

They are wrong. It takes only a moment of extreme thirst to attain such a state. And the ineffable instant when the parched man raises a glass of water to his lips: that is God.

It is an instant of absolute love and boundless wonder. Whosoever has this experience is bound to be pure and noble for as long as it lasts. I came to teach that fervor, nothing else. My message is so simple as to be disconcerting.

It is so simple that it is doomed to fail. The excess of simplicity obstructs understanding. One must experience a mystical trance in order to attain the splendor which the human mind, in normal circumstances, qualifies as indigence. The good news is that extreme thirst makes for an ideal mystical trance.

I advise prolonging it. Those who thirst should delay the moment of drinking. Not indefinitely, of course. The point is not to endanger one's health. I am not asking for a meditation on one's thirst, I am asking that it be deeply experienced, body and soul, before it is quenched.

Try this experiment: after dying of thirst for a good long while, don't drink your glass of water all in one go. Take a single sip and keep it in your mouth for a few seconds before swallowing. Notice how wonderful it feels. That dazzling moment is God.

I repeat, this is not a metaphor for God. The love you feel in that precise moment for your sip of water *is* God. It is I who am able to feel this love for everything that exists. That is what it means to be Christ.

Up to now, it has not been easy. Tomorrow, it will be excruciatingly difficult. Therefore, in order to succeed, I have made a decision which will help me: I will not drink any water from the pitcher the jailer has left in my cell.

It makes me sad. I would have liked, one last time, to know that supreme sensation, the one I prefer above all. I have deliberately decided to forgo it. Which is unwise: dehydration will be a handicap when it comes time for me to carry the cross. But I possess enough self-awareness to know that my thirst will protect me. It can become so great that all other suffering will be deadened.

I must try to get some sleep. I lie down on the floor of the jail, which is dirtier than bare earth. I've learned to be indifferent to foul smells. All I have to do is remind myself that nothing smells bad on purpose—I don't know if it's true, but in any event, this reasoning helps me to put up with even the worst stench.

I've always been amazed at how, when we lie down, we can let the weight of our body go. Even though I don't weigh much, what a deliverance! Incarnation means carrying this baggage of flesh around with me. In this day and age, plump people have the ascendancy. Not a model for me, I'm thin: you cannot be stout and then proclaim you are there on behalf of the poor. Madeleine thinks I'm handsome, but she's the only one. My own mother moans when she sees me, "Eat, you look pitiful!"

I eat as little as possible. If I had to carry more than the hundred and twenty pounds I weigh, I'd be out of breath. I've noticed that quite a few people won't listen to me because I'm so thin. In their eyes I read, "How can anyone find wisdom in such a beanpole?"

That is also why I chose Peter as my commander: he may be less inspired than John and less faithful than just any old stranger, but he has the features of a colossus. When he speaks, people are impressed. On top of it, that's true for me, too. Although I know he will deny me, he inspires so much trust. It's not just that he's tall and well built. I love watching him eat. He doesn't pick at his food, he grabs hold of it and gobbles it down, no simpering, with all the rough enjoyment of a brave man. He drinks straight from the pitcher, emptying it in one go, then he burps and wipes his mouth with the back of his strong hand. It's not an act, he hasn't noticed that other people have a different way of eating. You can't help but love him.

As for John, he eats the way I do. I don't know if he is seeking to imitate my own parsimony. Either way, it means my affection has to be kept at a distance. What a strange species we are! Nothing human is foreign to me. When I'm eating, I have to stop myself from saying to him, "Go ahead, eat, you get on our nerves with your manners!" It's all the more absurd in that I behave like that myself.

For me to love John, I have to leave the table. When he's walking next to me, listening to me, I love him. I've been assured that I'm a good listener. I don't know what sort of effect that has on people, to have me listen to them. I do know that the way John listens is pure love, and it's thrilling.

When I talk to Peter, he opens his eyes wide and listens for a minute. Then I see his attention begin to falter. It's not his fault, he doesn't realize, his gaze darts around looking for a place to settle. The moment I speak to John, he lowers his gaze slightly, as if he knows that what I am about to share with him in confidence will move him, even trouble him. When I stop talking, he remains silent for a little while then looks up at me again, his eyes shining.

Madeleine, too, listens to me like that. It is less astonishing, for an unfair reason: in this era of mine, women are taught to listen in this way. And yet, the ones who actually listen closely are few and far between. How I wish I could spend this last night with her! She used to say, "Let our sleep be the sleep of wild passion." Then she would curl up next to me and fall asleep at once. I've never been a sound sleeper, so it was as if she were sleeping for both of us.

Thanks to her, I discovered that sleeping is an act of love. When we slept like that, our souls mingled even more than when we were making love. It was a long disappearance that took us away together. When at last I sank into sleep, it was with the exquisite sensation of being shipwrecked.

My illusion was confirmed upon awakening. I had lost my bearings to such a degree that our bed had become the shore where we had washed up, and where we were amazed to find we had survived. The gratitude of waking up on the beach, next to one's beloved!

So powerful was this impression of having survived that the dawning day was bound to bring its share of joy. The first embrace, the first word of love, the first sip.

If there was a river nearby, Madeleine would suggest going for a dip. "There is no better way to start the morning," she said. Nothing like it, indeed, to wash away the smells of too good a night.

"Make sure you quench your thirst while we're there," she added, "because I'll have nothing better to offer you."

We never had any sort of breakfast. The thought of eating the moment you get out of bed has always turned my stomach. I can't believe it has become customary. But a few sips of water were just the thing to refresh one's breath.

These delightful thoughts have no hypnagogic power. If I really want to fall asleep, I have to force myself to feel bored. It takes an iron will to be deliberately bored. Alas, perhaps it's the imminence of death: nothing seems boring to me now—even the speeches of the Pharisees, which used to make my eyes turn glassy, now seem comical. I try to recall Joseph's attempts to teach me the art of woodworking. I was such a bad pupil! And how disconcerted Joseph would look, he who never got angry!

*

Christ means gentle. The irony of it is that my human parents are a thousand times gentler than I am. They found each other: creatures of such similar goodness, it's enough to make you discouraged. I can see straight into people's hearts, I know when they're good simply because they're making an effort—that, by the way, was often my own attitude. Joseph was good by nature. I was at his side when he was dying, he did not even curse the stupid accident that cost him his life, but smiled at me and said:

"Mind you don't let this happen to you, too."

And he died.

No, Joseph, I will not die falling off a roof.

Mother arrived too late.

"He didn't suffer," I said.

She stroked his face tenderly. My parents were not in love with each other, but they loved each other very much.

My mother, too, is a far better person than I am. Evil is completely foreign to her, so much so that she doesn't see it when it's right there in front of her. I envy her ignorance. I am not unacquainted with evil. In order for me to be able to spot it in other people, I have had to have some in myself as well.

I do not lament the fact. Were it not for this dark streak inside me, I could never have fallen in love. Falling in love does not lie in wait for creatures unversed in evil. Not that there is anything evil about love, but to fall in love, one must have those deep abysses to accommodate its profound dizziness.

This does not mean I am a bad man, nor that Madeleine is a bad woman. The dark streak was not active within us. More so for Madeleine than for me, of course. She would never have flown into a rage with the merchants at the Temple. Even if the cause was just, what a terrible memory I have of that anger! A sensation of venom spreading through my blood, ordering me to throw those people out, all that shouting; I hated every moment of it.

Fortunately, right now, I feel nothing of the sort. Even at my trial, when I heard those repulsive testimonies, my anger was not aroused. Indignation is a different fire, it does not cause such abominable suffering. If I managed to keep my scorn to myself, it is because scorn, unlike anger, is not explosive in nature.

Jesus, you won't get any sleep, going on like this. You have no willpower!

I just woke up.

So, I did nod off after all. A moment of grace. I thank God, reflecting all the while that this really does take the cake, to be thanking him today of all days. But the fact remains: I got some sleep.

I can sense the sweetness of rest flowing through my veins. All it takes is a few minutes of sleep to feel this sensual delight. I savor it, knowing very well that it is for the last time.

I will never wake up again.

A poet, whose name I do not know, will say in the future, "All the pleasure of days is in their mornings." I share this opinion. I like mornings. There is an inexorable power to that time of day. Even if the most terrible things have happened the day before, there is a purity to mornings.

I feel clean. I am not. My soul is clean this morning. The scorn I was feeling yesterday has vanished. I don't want to rejoice too soon, yet I have the sudden conviction that I will die without hatred. I hope I'm not mistaken.

A final pee in a corner of the jail, then I lie back down and lo and behold, a miracle: it's raining.

It's the wrong time of year for rain. I find myself hoping it will last. They would have to cancel the show: a crucifixion in the rain would be a total flop; the audience would desert. The Romans need their tortures to draw crowds, otherwise they worry there is disapproval. They think if the people get entertainment, they won't care about politics. Bad weather pays no heed to circumstances, but Rome has ears that can hear great distances: to crucify three men without the commoners turning up en masse would be considered a snub.

I've always loved the feeling of being sheltered the moment it starts raining harder and harder. It's a wonderful sensation. Somewhat foolishly, we associate it with serenity. In truth, it is a moment of pleasure. The sound of rain requires a roof for a sound box: to be under that roof is the best place to enjoy the concert. A delightful score, changing subtly, rhapsodic without showing off: any common downpour has something of a blessing about it.

Now it's becoming more of a deluge. I imagine a different fate. The authorities are fleeing the rising waters. They let me go. I return to my province, I marry Madeleine, we lead the simple life of ordinary people. Having been a mediocre carpenter, I turn to sheep herding. We make cheese with the ewe's milk. Every evening, our children delight in it and they grow like plants. We grow old and happy.

Am I tempted? Yes. When I was younger, I rejoiced in being the chosen one. Now I no longer have that hunger, it has been sated. I would rather return to the sweetness of anonymity, wrongfully known as banality. And yet, there is nothing more extraordinary than a shared life. I love everyday life. Its repetitiveness allows one to deepen the sparkling moments of day and night: eating bread fresh from the oven, walking barefoot on the ground still damp with dew, filling one's lungs with fresh air, lying next to one's beloved—how could anyone want anything else?

That life, too, ends with death. I suppose, all the same,

that dying is very different when it is the work of time: you die surrounded by your loved ones; it must be like falling asleep. If I could avoid this violence foretold, I could wish for nothing better.

The rain has stopped. My exquisite what-if has come to an end.

All will come to pass.

"Accept it," whispers a kindly voice inside my head.

A wise man from Asia has suggested that hope and fear are the two sides of a same feeling, and that is why one must give up both of them. It makes sense: I have known hope—in vain, and now my terror is so much greater. However, the message that sends me to my death will not condemn hope. Perhaps it is a chimera, but the love that pours from me contains a hopefulness that has no counterpart in fear.

All the same, I will have to endure infinite suffering. "Accept it." Do I have any choice? I accept it, if only to suffer less.

T hey have come for me at last.

I give a sigh of relief. The worst is behind me. It's no longer just a matter of waiting for the ordeal.

I am quickly disillusioned. Now the show has begun. They've placed a crown of thorns on my head, pressing it down to make my scalp bleed. I'm sorry to say that ridicule does not kill.

I am publicly flogged. I cannot see the point of this spectacle. You could swear it's some sort of appetizer. Before the main course, the crucifixion, there's nothing like a little flogging to whet the appetite. Every crack of the whip leaves me stiff with pain. The kindly voice in my head repeats that I must accept. Just behind it, a grating voice resounds, "The fun and games have only just begun." I stifle a nervous laugh which might be taken for insolence. It's a pity I'm not supposed to be impertinent, that would amuse me.

I refuse to dwell on the fact that the whip is tearing me apart with pain: what lies ahead will be even more painful. And to think it's actually possible to suffer even more than this!

There are some spectators, but not that many. This is for the happy few: they've been hand-picked, connoisseurs who can appreciate what they're seeing. They seem to find the cast first-rate: the torturer excels at his flogging, the victim is modest, a most tasteful performance. Thank you, Pontius Pilate, your receptions continue to live up to their reputation.

If you don't mind, we won't stay for the next round of festivities, which is bound to be more vulgar.

A blazing sun greets me outside. Did they flog me for that long? The morning has gone by. My eyes take several minutes to adjust to the glare. Suddenly, I see the crowd. Now there really is a crush. There are so many people you can hardly tell them apart. They share a single, avid gaze. They don't want to lose a single crumb of the spectacle.

Not a trace of the night's cool rain lingers in the air. The ground, however, still attests to its passage: it's as muddy as it gets. I stare at the cross leaning against the wall. I mentally calculate its weight. Will I be able to carry it? Will I manage?

Absurd questions: I have no choice. Whether I'm able to or not, I'll have to do it.

They bring the cross to me. It's so heavy I could collapse. I am staggered. There's no way around it. How will I manage?

To walk as quickly as possible: that's the only way. Fat chance: my legs are like jelly. Every step requires an unthinkable effort. I work out the distance to Mount Calvary. It's impossible. I'll die long before I get there. It's almost good news, I won't be crucified.

And yet, I know I will be. I really will have to hold out. Come on, don't think about it, there's no point, keep going. If only I weren't sinking into the mud, which makes the cross twice as heavy!

It doesn't help matters when people start pushing toward me as I go by. I hear the most extraordinary comments:

"Not acting so clever, now, are we?"

"If you are a magician, why don't you get yourself out of this?"

The positive side is that I don't have it in me to despise them. I don't think about it. All my energy has been requisitioned for my burden.

Don't fall. It's forbidden. Moreover, if you fall, you'll have to get back up. It will be worse. Yes, there are ways for it to be worse. Don't fall, I beg of you.

I feel like I'm about to fall. It's a matter of seconds. There's nothing I can do, there are limits, and I'm reaching them. There, I have fallen. The cross has knocked me down, I've got my nose in the mud. At least this gives me a few seconds of deliverance. I savor this strange freedom; I enjoy the pleasure of my weakness. Naturally, the blows instantly rain down on me, I practically don't feel them, since it hurts all over.

Off we go, once again, I lift up the monstrous weight. I'm on my feet again, staggering, and now I know the cost. Matthew, 11:30, "For my yoke is easy and my burden is light." Not for me, my friends. The word of God is not addressed to me, here. But that I knew. To experience it is different. My entire being protests. What enables me to go on is that voice I identify with the husk, and which murmurs, constantly, "Accept it."

I thought I had touched bottom, but there stands my mother. No. Don't look at me, please. Alas, I see that you see, and that you understand. Your eyes are wide with horror. It's beyond pity, you are living through what I am living through, only worse, because it's always worse when it's your own child. It's against nature to die before your own mother. If on top of it she is present during my torture, there can be nothing more cruel.

This is not a final, beautiful moment, it is the ugliest of moments. I don't have the strength to tell her to go away, and even if I did, she wouldn't listen. My dear mother, I love you, don't watch your son suffering like a dog, look away from what I am enduring. If only you could faint, mother!

My father, who never answers my prayers, has strange

ways of showing me—how to put it—not his solidarity, let alone his compassion, so under the circumstances, I see no other word for it than this: his existence. The Romans are beginning to realize that I will not make it alive to Mount Calvary. For them, this would be a bitter defeat: what's the point of crucifying a dead man? So, they have stopped a man on his way back from his fields, a cocky fellow who happened to be passing by.

"You've been requisitioned. Help this condemned man to carry his burden."

Even though he has received an order, the man is a miracle. He doesn't give it a second thought, he sees a stranger staggering under a burden that is too heavy for him, and, without further ado, he helps me.

He helps me!

All my life, this has never happened. I didn't know what it was like. Someone is helping me. Never mind why.

I could weep. In that abject species that doesn't give a damn about me and for whom I'm sacrificing myself, there is this man who hasn't come to enjoy the show, and who, I can tell, is helping me with all the goodness of his heart.

If he'd just shown up on the street by chance and seen me staggering under the cross, I think he would have reacted in exactly the same way: not pausing to think for even a second, he would have run up to help. There are people like that. They don't know how rare they are. If we asked Simon of Cyrene why he behaves this way, he wouldn't understand the question: he doesn't know that you can be any other way.

My father created a strange species: they're either bastards with opinions, or generous souls who do not think. In the state I'm in, I'm not thinking, either. I've discovered that I have a friend in Simon: I've always loved strong, sturdy people. They're never the ones who cause a problem. It suddenly feels as if the cross doesn't weigh a thing.

"Let me carry my share," I tell him.

"Honestly, it's easier if you let me do it," he replies.

I don't mind. But the Romans aren't having it. Simon is a good sort, and he tries to explain his point of view:

"This cross isn't heavy. If anything, the condemned man is getting in my way."

"The condemned man has to carry his burden," a soldier shouts.

"I don't understand. Do you want me to help him, or don't you?"

"You're a pain in the ass. Get the hell out!"

Sheepish, Simon looks at me as if to imply he's put his foot in it. I smile at him. It was too good to be true.

"Thank you," I say.

"Thank *you*," he says, oddly.

He looks almost upset.

There's no time for a proper farewell. I have to keep moving ahead, dragging this dead weight. And I've noticed something I could not have predicted: the cross is not as heavy now. It is still horrific, but the episode with Simon has changed things. It's as if my friend took away with him the most inhuman part of my burden.

This miracle—because it is a miracle—has nothing to do with me. Find me a more extraordinary form of magic in the Scriptures. You will seek in vain.

It's unbearably hot. My eyebrows are no longer doing their job, the sweat on my brow is trickling into my eyes, I can't see where I'm going. The Romans guide me with the crack of their whips; it's as brutal as it is ineffective. I didn't know it was possible to sweat this much. How can there be so much water and salt in me?

And suddenly, a cloth sets me free: a piece of fabric as soft as it is delightful passes over my face in a silky caress. Who can be making such a gesture? Someone as kind as Simon of Cyrene, but that tall beanpole would not be able to wipe my face so delicately.

I don't want it to stop, and, at the same time, I'd like to know who this kindly soul is. The cloth is withdrawn, and I find myself looking at the loveliest woman on earth. She seems as stunned as I am.

The instant is frozen, time is suspended, I no longer know who I am or what I am doing here, none of it matters, there are these big, pure eyes looking at me, I have no more past or future, the world is perfect, let nothing move, we are in the imminence of the ineffable. This is what they mean by love at first sight, something colossal is about to happen, some high-brow music is missing from our desire, but this time we shall hear it at last.

"My name is Veronica," she says.

It's amazing how beautiful the voice of an unknown woman can be.

The crack of the whip brings me back to reality. Once again, the cross is crushing me, I drag myself forward, I'm back in hell.

Still, since the moment this torture began, fate has been hounding me, everything has come tumbling down on me, best and worst, I have found friendship, I have found love, I can scarcely get over it. Veronica—who could she be?—the music of her voice still echoing in my ears, and I have discovered that a melody can lighten the world, and a bright face can give you the strength to carry the instrument of your own torture.

On this planet, there are the likes of Simon of Cyrene and Veronica. Two incomparable examples of sublime courage.

I have returned to my century. I am struggling. Where will I find the energy not to collapse again? Some part of my brain is envisioning the moment of the accident. My eyes can see the place where it will happen. I bargain with myself, "Just one more step . . . just another half a step . . ."

Falling is an illusion of repose. And still, I savor this second fall. It feels so good to surrender to the law of gravity. A hail of lashes falls upon me at once, the sweet sensation lasts only a second, but in the state I'm in, every second counts.

It feels as if I have been carrying, dragging this cross for hours. That can't be right. I'm finding it hard to recall my former life. Since I embarked on the way to Calvary, I've been dazzled first by a man, then by a woman. I saw my mother again, too. It has often been said that I liked women better. To prefer one sex over the other would, in my opinion, be a sign of disregard.

The daughters of Jerusalem crowd around me, weeping. I try to get them to dry their tears:

"Come now, it's just a bad spell to get through, it will all work out."

I don't believe a word I'm saying. It won't work out, it will only get worse. It's just that their sobs won't let me breathe. How can we help someone? Certainly not by crying in front of them. Simon helped me, Veronica helped me. Neither one of them was crying. Nor did they have grins on their faces: they were taking concrete steps.

No, I do not prefer women. I think they protect me. I cannot attribute that to anything other than the sweetness of my behavior toward them, which is not normal practice among men in these parts.

Need I point out that I do not prefer men, either? There are certain verbs I avoid, such as prefer, or replace—people have no idea how alike these verbs are. I've seen people fight in order to be preferred, never realizing that this merely makes them replaceable.

One day, people will claim that no one is irreplaceable.

That is the contrary of my message. The love that consumes me asserts that every individual is irreplaceable. It is appalling to know in advance that my ordeal is serving no purpose.

That's not altogether true. A few individuals will understand. I cannot rule out the fact that they won't need my sacrifice for that. I'll never know. Better not to let it fill me with bitterness, which would only make my fate even more terrible.

Strange thoughts come to you when you are dragging a cross along like this. It's an exaggeration to call them thoughts, they are merely snatches, short-circuits. What I am carrying is far too heavy for me. I have never felt so wretched.

It's a pity I did not know this sooner: to carry only a light burden is sufficient as an ideal in life. An incredible lesson which will be of no use to me. I recall spending entire days on the road, congratulating myself on my happiness over nothing. I wasn't happy over nothing. I was savoring lightness.

I have collapsed for the third time. Biting the dust has acquired its full meaning. The ground isn't muddy now, the sun has dried the earth. I can see the top of Mount Calvary. Why am I in a hurry to get there? I find it hard to believe I'll suffer any more on the cross than under it, as I do now.

It's a common experience: when you climb a mountain, first you look at it from below, where it doesn't seem so high. You have to get to the top to realize just how high it is. Calvary is just a little mound, but it feels as if this climbing will never end.

I don't know how I managed to get back to my feet. As things stand, everything is an effort, I'm aching all over. I must be solid, since I haven't passed out. The last steps are the worst, I cannot feel the joy of having overcome an ordeal, I know that what is about to begin here is of another nature altogether.

They waste no time proving this to me in the simplest way: they stripped off my clothing. It was only a robe of linen and a belt: now I appreciate just what those rags were worth.

As long as you are dressed, you are someone. Now I'm no one. I'm nothing at all anymore. A little voice in my head whispers, "They left you your loincloth. It could be worse." The entire human condition can be summed up like that: it could be worse.

I don't dare look at the two men who are already on their crosses. I will spare them the pain of being stared at, something I have just experienced myself at length.

One of the two sneers at me, "If you are the son of God, ask your father to get you out of this."

I sincerely admire the fact that, in his situation, he hasn't lost his sarcastic wit.

I hear the other one saying, "Quiet, he deserves this less than we do."

He's suffering to this degree and is still eager to defend me—I am touched. I thank the man.

No, I didn't tell him that he was saved. To say such a thing to someone who is going through such an ordeal would be playing games. And to tell one of the crucified men, "You are saved," and not the other would have been the height of pettiness and cynicism.

I'm pointing out these issues because this is not what will be written in the Gospels. Why not? I don't know. The evangelists were nowhere near me when this happened. And regardless of what people have said, they didn't know me. I'm not angry with them, but nothing is more irritating than those people who, under the pretext that they love you, claim that they know you inside out.

In truth, I felt the pull of fraternal love toward those two crucified men for the simple reason that I was about to share their ordeal. Someday someone will come up with the expression "affirmative action" to suggest what might have been my attitude toward the man we will call the good thief. I have no opinion on the matter, I just know the two men moved me, each in his own way. For while I loved what the good thief said to me, I also loved the pride of the bad one—who wasn't actually bad. I don't see what's so bad about stealing a loaf of bread, and I can understand why someone might not feel remorse in such a situation.

The time has come: I am lying on the cross. What I carried will henceforth be carrying me. I see the nails and hammers coming. I'm so frightened that I find it hard to breathe. They nail my feet and my hands. It doesn't take long, I hardly have time to realize. And then they raise my cross between my brothers'.

Now I feel this incredible pain for the first time. To have nails through my palms was nothing compared to having my weight upon them, and what is true for my hands is a thousand times worse for my feet. The rule is, above all, don't move. The slightest movement increases what is already unbearable pain.

I tell myself I'll get used to it, that my nerves cannot go on feeling something this horrific for long. But I find out that they most certainly can, and that this equipment of mine can record the most infinitesimal variations as well as the most enormous.

To think that when I was dragging this cross, I believed that the purpose of life was to avoid carrying any heavy burdens! The meaning of life is to avoid pain. That's it.

There's no way out of this. I am entirely absorbed by my pain. No thoughts, no memories can set me free.

I look at the people looking at me. "What's it like, this thing you're going through?" That's what I read in countless gazes, both compassionate and cruel. If I had to answer them, I couldn't find the words.

I'm not holding it against the cruel ones. For a start, because all my faculties have been monopolized by my pain, and then, because if my pain can bring someone pleasure, it's better that way.

Madeleine has come. I didn't like seeing my mother, but it moves me to see my beloved. She is so beautiful that compassion cannot disfigure her. My suffering is so great that my soul cries out, even if my lips are silent, unable to imagine a fitting cry.

The cry in my soul penetrates Madeleine. This is not a metaphor. Is it a surfeit of pain or death approaching? I see Madeleine's love in the form of rays. The word ray is not quite right, it's both more delicate and rounder, more concentric, she emanates a luminous wave, and I receive it, and it's as gentle as what I give her is painful.

I can see this howling in my soul, or rather my soul in the form of a furious current going to meet Madeleine's loving soul and mingling with it. And it gives me, if not a sense of lightening, a very mysterious joy.

My thirst, which I had kept as a secret weapon, now sends me a reminder. An excellent idea. The extreme torment of my throat enables me to emerge from the horror of my lacerated body; there is some concrete salvation in this alteration.

The wave that links me to Madeleine is an oblique one, and this slant owes less to my raised position than to the nature of its blue light. My beloved and I secretly exult over what we alone know.

And when I say alone, this means that my father doesn't know. He has no body, and the absolute nature of the love that Madeleine and I share at this moment rises from the body the way music flows from an instrument. You only learn such powerful truths when you are thirsty, when you experience love, and when you are dying: three activities that require a body. Naturally the soul, too, is indispensable for this, but in no way can it suffice.

It's enough to make you laugh. I don't risk it, it might bring on a spasm of pain. If I really do have to die, under no circumstances must I die laughing. I'm horribly afraid of ruining my death. This pain is so extreme that I might even miss the great moment.

What a blunder this crucifixion is. My father's intent was to show how far one could go out of love. If his plan had been no more than just silly, it could remain pointless. Unfortunately, it's so noxious that it's terrifying. Masses of men will embrace martyrdom because of my foolish example. And if only it had stopped there! Even people wise enough to choose a simple life will be contaminated. Because this thing my father is inflicting on me is proof of such deep scorn for the body that something of it will always remain.

Father, you have just been surpassed by your invention. You could take pride in the fact, proof of your creative genius. But instead, under the guise of giving an edifying lesson of love, you have staged this punishment, the most hideous imaginable, heaviest with consequence.

It did start off well, for all that. To engender a solidly incarnated son, now there was a good story; you could have learned a lot from it, if only you had really sought to understand what you have failed to understand. You are God: what does this pride mean to you? Is it even pride? Pride in itself is not a bad thing. No, I see a ridiculous trait therein: susceptibility.

Yes, you are susceptible. Another sign of this: you won't be able to stand the various forms that revelation will take. You will be offended when men from opposite ends of the earth, or from just next door, seek to experience their verticality in a number of fashions. Occasionally with human sacrifices, which you will have the nerve to find barbaric!

Father, why are you behaving in such a petty way? Am I being blasphemous? It's true. Punish me, then. Can you punish me even more?

Yes, you can: now my pain is a thousand times greater. Why are you doing this? I'm criticizing you. Have I said that I didn't love you? I am full of resentment, you make me angry. Love allows such feelings. What would you know about love?

That really is the problem. You don't know love. Love is a story, you need a body to tell it. What I have just said makes no sense to you. If only you were aware of your own ignorance!

The pain has become so intense that I hope I'll die very soon. Alas, I know I'm still long for this world. The flame of life has not flickered. Above all, I must stay still; the slightest movement comes with a price that is beyond thinkable. Here's something else that is awful about indignation: it makes you squirm. Those who are indignant cannot stay still.

Accept it, my friend. Yes, that's me I'm talking to. Extend your friendship to yourself, that's what's needed. Love would be unpleasant: love overdoes it, and that's bad for your health. Hatred is the same, but even more unjust. I am my friend, and I'm fond of the man I am.

Accept it, not because it's acceptable, but because you will suffer less. Not accepting is fine when it's of some use: in this case it will serve no purpose.

Haven't you hit the trifecta, in a way? You've summed up the three most radical situations: thirst, love, and death. You are at the intersection of all three. Make the most of it, my friend. What an abject expression. But I can't go saying, "rejoice in it," it would sound like I'm making fun of myself.

These are the facts: what I am living through is life-changing, there's no mistaking it. I cannot put this suffering to one side, therefore I've immersed myself in thirst, in order that I might, if not escape it, at least sidestep it.

What grandiose thirst! A masterpiece of alteration. My

tongue has been transformed into pumice stone, and when I rub it against my palate, it's abrasive. Explore your thirst, my friend. This is a journey, it is leading you to a source, how lovely it is, have you heard it, yes, it's the right song, hearken to it, there is some music that is worth it, this tender murmur makes me happy right to my core, I have this taste of stone in my mouth. There will be a country so poor that in their language, to drink and to eat will be one and the same verb, to be used with extreme parsimony, to drink is a bit like eating liquid pebbles—no, that only works if the water is oozing, and in my journey, it's not oozing, it's gushing, I am lying in such a way that I can make contact with the water, it loves me the way it loves the chosen source. Drink me without limits, my love, may your thirst fulfill you and never be quenched, since that word does not exist in any language.

Is it any surprise that thirst leads to love? Loving always begins by drinking with someone. Perhaps because no other sensation disappoints so little. A dry throat imagines water as ecstasy, and the oasis is proof against waiting. He who drinks after crossing the desert never says, "It's not all it's cracked up to be." To offer a drink to the woman you are about to love is to suggest that the delight will be at least as great as the expectation.

I became incarnate in a country of drought. Not only was it imperative that I be born in a place where thirst reigns supreme, but it also had to be a hot place.

From the little I know of the cold, it would have skewed everything. Not only does it numb thirst, it also eliminates all additional sensation. If you're cold, you're cold and nothing else. If you're dying from the heat, you are perfectly capable of suffering from a thousand other things at the same time.

I'm still damned alive. I'm sweating—where is all this liquid coming from? My blood is circulating, pouring from my wounds, could the pain be any worse? It hurts so much that the geography of my skin has been altered, it feels as if the most sensitive zones of my body are now located in my arms and shoulders, this position is intolerable, to think that one day a human being came up with the idea of crucifixion, clever thinking, proof of my father's failure: it is one of his creatures who dreamt up this torture.

Love thy neighbor as thyself. A sublime teaching, and I am in the process of professing the contrary. I have accepted this monstrous, humiliating, indecent, interminable execution: whoever accepts such a thing does not love himself.

I can take refuge behind paternal error. Because his plan was nothing more than a blunder, pure and simple. But how could I have been so mistaken? Why did I not realize until I was on the cross? I had my suspicions, to be sure, but not to the point of rejecting the matter entirely.

The excuse that comes to mind is that I behaved the way anyone would have: I lived from one day to the next without giving much thought to the consequences. I like the version where I was merely a man—and how I enjoyed being one!

Alas, I cannot close my eyes; there was something else that was worse than submitting to my father, something worse than anything. The friendship I granted myself a short while ago has come too late. If I have accepted the unspeakable, it is not solely by virtue of an exonerating unconsciousness, it is because I carry inside me that ordinary poison: self-hatred.

How did I get it? I have tried to go back through my memories. As soon as I knew what I was destined for, I hated myself. But I can recall memories from before memories, snatches where I did not say *I*, where I was not yet aware, and I did not hate myself.

I was born innocent, then something was ruined, I don't know how. I'm accusing no one but myself. It's a strange sin one commits at around the age of three. To accuse oneself of it increases self-hatred, an additional absurdity. There is a flaw in creation.

And so, like everyone, I am holding my father responsible for my failure. This annoys me. Damned suffering! If there were no suffering, would we always go looking for a guilty party?

Laborer of the eleventh hour, I have been trying at last to become my own friend. I must forgive myself for having gone so seriously astray. The hardest thing is to convince myself of my own ignorance. Did I really not know?

A voice inside assures me that I did know. But how could I have? Self-hatred is terrible, but there I was, preaching, "Love thy neighbor as thyself," and now I am forced to see the logic: how could I have hated others? And hate them to such a degree?

So, was this atrocious comedy nothing but the work of the devil?

Oh, I've had my fill of him. The moment things go wrong, there is talk of the devil. It's too easy. From where I am now, I can allow myself every form of blasphemy: I don't believe in the devil. There's no point in believing in him. There's enough evil on earth without adding another layer.

The people watching my ordeal are mostly what are commonly

referred to as good people, and I'm saying this without the slightest irony. I look into their eyes, and I can see more than enough evil on which to found not only my misadventure but all those past and future. Even Madeleine's gaze contains some. As does mine. I don't know my own gaze, yet I know what's inside me: I have accepted my fate, I don't need any other signs.

To reject this explanation and call Devil that which is only latent meanness, is to adorn pettiness with a grandiose word, and thus endow it with a far greater power. One day, a wonderful woman will say, "I do not fear Satan half so much as I fear those who fear him." That's it in a nutshell.

Others will say that if you baptize goodness with God's name, you are bound to baptize evil as well. Where did you come up with the idea that God is goodness? Do I look like I am goodness? Is my father, who dreamt up this thing I have accepted, credible in his role? He hasn't claimed to be, by the way. He says he is love. Love is not goodness. The two might overlap, but then again, not always.

And even what he says he is—is he really? The power of love is sometimes so difficult to differentiate from all the other ambient currents. My father sent me here out of love for his creation. Find me a more perverse act of love.

I'm not seeking to prove my innocence. At the age of thirty-three, I've had more than enough time to think about the villainy of this business. There's not a single way to justify it. According to legend, I have expiated the sins of all humanity that has gone before me. Even if this were true, what is to become of the sins of humanity to follow? I cannot plead ignorance, because I know what is going to happen. And even if I didn't know, what sort of an imbecile would you have to be to suspect otherwise?

Moreover, how can I believe that my torture will expiate anything? My boundless suffering has not erased any part of the suffering unfortunate souls before me have endured. The very thought of expiation, with its absurd sadism, makes me sick.

If I were a masochist, I would forgive myself. But I'm not: there's not one single iota of sensual delight in the horror I'm going through. And yet, I must forgive myself. In this jumble of words pouring from my thoughts, the only one that might save is: forgiveness. And now I'm offering a striking counterexample. Forgiveness requires no counterpart, it is just an impulse of the heart one must feel. How can I explain this in the midst of sacrificing myself? Imagine someone who, in his effort to convert people to vegetarianism, sacrifices a lamb: everyone would laugh in his face.

And that is precisely the situation I am in. Love thy neighbor as thyself, do not inflict upon him what you yourself could not bear, if he has behaved badly toward you, do not require his punishment, turn the page magnanimously. Illustration: I hate myself so much that I am inflicting this atrocity upon myself; my punishment is the price to pay for the mistakes that you have committed.

How did I end up in such a situation? It has gradually occurred to me that this accumulation of paralipsis is the height of an *a fortiori* argument: with the level of guilt that is mine, if I manage to forgive myself, then everything shall be accomplished.

Can I do it?

There are a thousand ways to envisage the deed. It is impossible to tell which is the most abominable. Let's take the one that will be official: I am sacrificing myself for the good of all. Appalling! A dying father calls his children to his bedside and says to them:

"My dear children, I've had a dog's life, never had a moment's pleasure, exercised a despicable trade, pinched every penny, and I did it all for you, so that you would be sure of a fine inheritance."

Anyone who dares refer to this conceit as love is a monster. And yet, that is the very conceit I uttered. Thus, I have made it official: this is the way to behave.

Let's take my mother. I will say it again, she is a better person than I. She is so good that she has not come here: she knows that her presence would only increase my suffering. Yet for all that, she is not unaware of what is happening to me. What she is going through is infinitely worse than what I am going through, with the colossal difference that she neither chose it nor accepted it. I am the one who is inflicting this pain upon my own mother.

Madeleine: she and I are joined. I am in love with her the way she is in love with me. What if we were to reverse reality: I stand there where she is, while she is crucified, and I know it is what she wanted.

"I shared a passionate love with you, and still, I have chosen to be tortured in public. I have good news, my love: you have the right to look at me."

I could go on like this for a long time. Below me, there are children in the crowd. Up to puberty, we are different, not exactly innocent, we are capable of harm, but we have no filter, we are on the same level with everything. In this very moment, these open creatures are being filled with this abject sight.

Can I forgive myself for this?

I use the word *this* on purpose. I refuse to say crucifixion. It's far too elegant and precious. What I'm experiencing is coarse and ugly. If at least I could be sure people would forget quickly! The most devastating thing is knowing that they're going to talk about this for ever and ever, and not in order to decry my fate. No other example of human suffering will be the subject of such colossal glorification. They'll thank me for this. They'll admire me for this. They'll believe in me for this.

For *this*, the very thing for which I cannot forgive myself. I am responsible for the greatest misinterpretation in history, which is also the most deleterious.

I cannot plead submission to my father. Where he's concerned, I've racked up my acts of disobedience. Starting with Madeleine: I had no right to sexuality or to being in love. With Madeleine, I did not hesitate to carry on regardless. And I was not punished.

Oh, come on, that's not true either. I'm a laughable idiot if I think I was entitled to impunity in overstepping my father's ban regarding Madeleine. In truth, I was punished in advance.

Or maybe my mistake was to believe that I was. I believed so fundamentally that I would be condemned that I could not imagine any other outcome.

Even if it's too late for all that, let's imagine.

In the Garden of Gethsemane, Madeleine would have come and joined me. With a few kisses, she would have convinced me to choose life. We would have run away together, we would have gone to live in a faraway country, unsullied by my reputation, and we would have enjoyed the wonderful life of ordinary people. Every night, I would have fallen asleep holding my wife in my arms, and every morning, I would have woken up at her side. No happiness can equal these imaginings.

The only thing wrong with this version is that I have made my choice depend on Madeleine. What was stopping me from coming up with the idea all on my own? All I had to do was find her and reach out to her. She would have followed me without hesitation.

I never even thought of it.

I certainly accomplished my share of miracles. Now I no

longer can. I'm in too much pain to reach the husk. I could only obtain the power of the husk through complete unconsciousness. This extreme pain blocks the way now. I swear that if I could perform one last miracle, I would set myself free from this cross.

You idiot visionary, are you going to stop hurting yourself? Yes, it's me I'm speaking to.

I have to forgive myself. Why can't I?

Because I'm thinking about it. The more I think about it, the less I forgive myself.

What's stopping me from forgiving is thinking.

I have to forgive myself without thinking. It depends solely on my decision, not on the horror of my act. I have to decide that it's done.

I was ten years old, playing with the other village children: we were jumping into the lake from the top of the overhang and I couldn't do it. One of the kids said, "You have to jump without thinking about it."

I managed to empty my mind, and I jumped. A long time went by before I landed in the water. I loved the exaltation of it.

I have to empty my mind, in the same way. Create a void where currently a great noise is plaguing me. What is pompously referred to as "thought" is nothing more than tinnitus.

There, I've done it.

I've forgiven myself.

It's done. It's a performative verb. No sooner said—as it must be said, in the absolute sense of the verb—than done.

I have just saved myself, and saved, therefore, everything that is. Does my father know this? Surely not. He's useless when it comes to doing things on the spur of the moment. It's not his fault: to be able to do things last minute, you have to have a body.

I still have one. Never have I been more incarnate than this: suffering has nailed me to my body. I am filled with conflicting emotions at the thought of leaving it. In spite of the intense pain, I have not forgotten what I owe this incarnation.

At least I have stopped my mental torture. It makes things considerably easier to be able to look deep in Madeleine's eyes: she can tell I've won. She nods.

How long have I been on this cross?

Madeleine's lips form words I cannot hear. As she is speaking to me, I can see a golden arc of words coming in my direction. The crackling of sparks lasts longer than her sentence, and their impact goes deep in my chest.

Fascinated, I follow her example. I utter inaudible words, addressed to her, I see them leaving me in the form of a golden beam, and I know she is taking them in.

Everyone else still has that pitying look. They don't get it. It must be said that the nature of my victory is tenuous.

I'm not dead yet. How can I hold on until the end?

Strange as it may seem, I can tell that I might collapse, which means I'm not dead yet.

In order to avoid collapsing, I resort to the good old method: pride. The sin of pride? If you like. At this stage, my sin seems so ridiculous that I have already forgiven myself for it.

Yes, pride: in this moment, I am filling a space that will become the obsession of humankind for millennia. The fact that it is a misinterpretation changes nothing.

It shall be given to one person alone to have this observation post, not because I am the last man in our species to be crucified—how lovely that would be—but because no other crucifixion will ever have such a resounding impact. My father chose me for this role. It was a mistake, a monstrous thing to do, but it will remain one of the most extraordinarily moving stories of all time. It will be called the Passion of Christ.

A judicious name: a passion signifies something one is subjected to and therefore, semantically, a surfeit of feeling in which reason plays no part.

It was not wrong of my father to assign this role to me. I admit as much. I have been capable of enough blindness to be mistaken on this point, enough love to forgive myself, and enough pride to keep my head held high.

I committed the greatest of sins. It will have immeasurable consequences. And there we are: it is in the nature of sin to have consequences. If I can forgive myself, then all those who will be greatly mistaken can forgive themselves.

"It is finished."

I said it. I realize this once I have spoken. Everyone has heard it.

My words cause panic. The sky darkens suddenly. I cannot get over the power of my words. I would like to speak some more, to unleash other phenomena, but I don't have the strength.

Luke will write that I said, "Father, forgive them, for they know not what they do." That's a misinterpretation. It was myself I had to forgive: I am more at fault than men are, and it was not from my father that I sought forgiveness.

I'm relieved I didn't say it: it would have been condescending towards men. Condescension is the type of scorn I loathe the most. And frankly, I'm in no position to scorn humanity.

Nor did I say to John (who was no more present at the time than the other disciples), "Behold thy mother," nor did I say to my mother (who showed the kindness of being absent), "Woman, behold thy son." John, I love you very much. But that does not mean you can go around spouting nonsense. At the same time, it hardly matters.

I have to spare my strength: I've reached the stage where speaking is at last having the desired effect. What linguistic performance am I hoping to accomplish?

The reply leaps to my heart. From deep within a desire wells up, the desire that most resembles me, my pet craving, my secret weapon, my true identity, the thing that has made me love life and makes me love it still:

"I thirst."

A stunning request. No one had thought of it. Really, that man who, for hours, has been suffering so greatly can still need something so ordinary? They find my entreaty as strange as if I had asked for a fan.

There's the proof that I've been saved: yes, despite the degree of pain I have reached, I can still find happiness in a sip of water. My faith is that intact.

Of all the words I have said on the cross, it is far and away the most important one, perhaps the only one that matters. When we leave childhood behind, we learn how to stave off hunger the moment it appears. No one teaches us how to defer the moment of quenching our thirst. When it comes, it is invoked as an indisputable emergency. We stop whatever we are doing to go and find something to drink.

I'm not being critical, drinking is a great delight. I'm just sorry that no one has explored the infinite nature of thirst, the purity of the impulse, the bitter nobility that is ours the moment we feel it.

John 4:14: "But whosoever drinketh of the water that I shall give him shall never thirst." Why did my favorite disciple come out with such a misinterpretation? The love of God is water that never quenches. The more we drink, the greater our thirst. At last, a pleasure that does not diminish desire!

Try it for yourself. Whatever your physical or mental concern might be, combine it with true thirst. Your quest will be all the sharper, more precise, enhanced. I'm not saying never drink, I'm just suggesting waiting a moment. There is so much to explore in thirst.

The joy of drinking, to start with, which is never celebrated enough. People make fun of Epicurus's words, "One glass of water and I die of pleasure." How wrong we are!

Verily I say unto you, nailed to the cross though I be, a glass of water would make me die of pleasure. I rather suspect I won't get one. I'm already proud that I can feel the desire, and glad to know that others besides me will experience the pleasure.

Obviously, no one imagined this scenario. There is no water on Mount Calvary. And even if there were, there would be no way of hoisting a cup up to my lips.

At the foot of the cross, I can hear a soldier telling his superior, "I have some water mixed with vinegar. Shall I give him some on a sponge?"

His superior allows him to do this, probably because he has no way of knowing how vital my request is. I shiver at the thought of feeling such a sensation one last time. I listen to the sound of the sponge soaking up the liquid: the sensual delight of it makes me weak with happiness. The soldier rams the sponge onto the tip of his spear and lifts it up to my mouth.

As exhausted as I am, I bite into the sponge and suck the juice. I'm elated. It is so good. That wonderful taste of vinegar. I suck at the sponge that is brimming with the sublime liquid, I drink, I am completely consumed by the delight of it. I don't waste a single drop.

"I have some more," says the soldier. "Shall I lift the sponge up to him again?"

His superior refuses, "That's enough."

Enough. What a terrible word! I say to you honestly: nothing is enough.

The superior has no greater grounds for refusing than he had for allowing. Command is a mysterious duty. I consider myself lucky to have been able to drink one last time, even if my thirst is far from quenched. I did what I set out to do.

The storm is about to break. People want me to die. I'm beginning to get fed up with this endless agony. I too would like to die quickly. It is not in my power to rush this demise.

The sky is torn asunder—thunder, lightning, downpour. The crowd scatters, dissatisfied, it's just as well it was for free, because he didn't even die, nothing happened.

I don't have the strength to stick my tongue out to catch the rain, but it moistens my lips, and I feel the inexpressible joy of breathing in the best fragrance in the world one last time, a fragrance which some day will be known by the fine name of petrichor.

Madeleine is still there before me, my death will be perfect, it is raining, and my gaze encounters that of the woman I love.

The great moment has arrived. My suffering has vanished,

my heart ceases to be clenched like a fist, and it receives a charge of love that surpasses everything, it's beyond pleasure, everything opens out onto infinity, there are no limits to this feeling of deliverance, the flower of death opening again and again and spreading its corolla.

The adventure has begun. I don't say, "My God, why hast thou forsaken me?" I thought of it, much earlier, but now I'm not thinking it, I'm not thinking anything, I have better things to do. My last words were, "I thirst."

I am allowed to enter the other world without leaving anything behind. It is a departure without separation. I am not torn from Madeleine. I am taking her love with me to that place where everything is beginning.

At last, my ubiquity has meaning: I am both in my body and outside it. I am too attached to my body not to leave some of my presence in it: the excruciating pain I felt over these last hours was not the best way to inhabit it. I don't feel amputated from my body; on the contrary, I feel as if I have regained some of its powers, such as access to the husk.

The soldier who gave me something to drink has seen that I am dead. He is a most discerning man: the difference is not obvious. He notifies his superior, who looks at me doubtfully. The moment amuses me: and if I were not completely dead, what would that change? Does this centurion have to believe in my magic to fear deception? Frankly, if I really wanted to resuscitate, I could not, for one simple reason: I'm exhausted. Dying is tiring.

The superior orders his soldier to pierce my heart with his spear. The unfortunate man is deeply upset, because he has grown fond of me: that spear whose sponge helped quench my thirst—he's loath to use it now in order to wound me.

The superior gets annoyed, demands to be obeyed at once. They have to verify whether I am dead: execute! The soldier aims his spear at my heart, deliberately avoids it, as if he wanted to spare that organ, and pierces me just below it. I'm not that well versed in anatomy to determine where he struck me; I feel the blade of his weapon inside me, but it doesn't hurt. A liquid flows out that is not blood.

Satisfied, the centurion announces:

"He is dead!"

The handful of individuals still standing below me walk away, heads lowered, both sorry and reassured. Most of them expected a miracle: the miracle did occur, although no one noticed. None of this was the least bit spectacular, it was an ordinary crucifixion; if there had not been a storm at the end, it really would have seemed as if the Eternal did not give a damn.

Madeleine runs to inform my mother:

"Your son suffers no more."

They fall into each other's arms. That part of me now flying above my body sees them and is moved.

Madeleine takes my mother's hand and leads her to Mount Calvary. The centurion has ordered the soldier and two other men to remove me from the cross, which is lying on the ground. They are kind enough to pull the nails from my hands and feet before detaching me, so that they won't be torn to shreds. I confess I am touched by their attentive gesture: I like my body, I don't want it to be mistreated any more than it has been already.

My mother asks them to return my body to her, and no one questions her right to it. Now that the Romans no longer doubt that I am dead, it is amazing how nice they've become. Who would think these are the same men who brutalized me all morning long? They seem sincerely touched by this woman who has come to ask for her son's remains.

I love this moment. My mother's embrace is extremely gentle, and these are our last moments together, I can feel her caress, her love; mothers who have lost a child need its body, precisely so that the child will not be lost.

Though I hated seeing my mother after I first fell under the weight of the cross, now I love being in her arms one last time. She is not weeping, you'd almost think she can sense this well-being of mine, she says the sweetest things to me, my little boy, my baby bird, my little lamb, she places kisses on my brow and my cheeks, I am trembling with emotion, and, oddly enough, I know she can tell. She doesn't seem sad; on the contrary. This thing they call my death has made her thirty-three years younger, how pretty she looks, my adolescent mother!

Dearest mother, what a privilege to be your son! A mother who has the gift of making her child know how much she loves him: that is absolute grace. I take in this headiness that is less common than you might think. I am swooning with pleasure.

What a strange state my body is in, dead to suffering but not to joy! I don't even know if I have access to the power of the husk—it's as if the miracle was springing spontaneously from it, my skin is alive, vibrant with happiness, and my mother gathers this quivering into her arms.

The descent from the cross is a scene that will inspire a multitude of artistic portrayals: the majority will depict this ambiguity. Mary almost always looks as if she has realized something out of the ordinary is happening, but she will not speak of it. As for my swooning, it is there every time.

This is spot-on: even the least mystical painters suspect that my death is a reward. My well-earned rest. Whether or not his soul has survived, how can we not sigh with relief on behalf of this unfortunate man whose torture has now ended?

Since I have access to works of art the world over, and for ever and ever, I like looking at the descents from the cross. I never so much as glance at scenes representing my crucifixion, nothing that reminds me of the torture. But I am very moved by those statues or paintings where I see my dead body in my mother's arms. The precision of the artists' gaze is striking.

Some of them, important ones at that, have captured my mother's sudden youthfulness. None of the texts mention it, probably because it's not meant to be important. The *mater dolorosa* has other fish to fry besides her wrinkles, I agree.

As a rule, it is the deceased who look younger on their deathbed. That is not the case where I'm concerned. Indeed, a crucifixion puts years on you. It looks as if my mother has been able to take advantage of the famous postmortem blush of youth. I like the way this links our two bodies.

On the *Pietà* at the entrance to Saint Peter's Basilica, Mary looks sixteen years old. I could be her father. The relationship has been so strikingly reversed that my mother has become my orphan.

Whatever the case may be, representations of the *mater dolorosa* are always hymns to love. The mother holding her child's body and seeming all the more enraptured, knowing it is for the last time.

She will be able to go and pray at his grave every day, but she knows that nothing can ever equal an embrace: yes, even with a dead body, all the love in the world is never better expressed than through a mother's embrace.

I am here. I have never stopped being here. In a different way, to be sure, but I am here.

There is no need to believe in anything in order to explore the mystery of presence. It is a common experience. How often are we here without being present? We don't necessarily know why this happens.

"Concentrate," we say to ourselves. What this means is "gather up your presence." When we talk of an unruly child, we are evoking the phenomenon of a scattered presence. Being distracted is all it takes.

Distraction was never my strong point. Maybe that's what it means to be Jesus: someone who is really and truly present.

It's hard for me to compare. I'm like others in that I only have my own experience to go on. What has been called my omniscience has left me with a vast ignorance.

The fact remains: a truly present person is not a very common sight. My trifecta—love, thirst, and death—also teaches three ways of being incredibly present.

When you fall in love, you become phenomenally present. Subsequently, it's not love that dissipates, but presence. If you want love to remain as strong as on the first day, you must cultivate your presence.

When you are thirsty, you're so present it's downright embarrassing. No need ramble on about that.

Dying is the show of presence par excellence. I cannot get over how many people hope they will die in their sleep. Their mistake is all the graver in that dying in your sleep is no guarantee you won't notice. And why would you want to miss out on the most interesting moment in your existence? Fortunately, no one dies without realizing, simply because that is impossible. Even the most distracted person will be abruptly called back to the present upon dying.

And afterwards? No one knows.

As for me, I can sense that I am here. Some people will assert that this is an illusion of my consciousness. However, everyone has noticed how very present the dead can be. Regardless of their faith. When someone dies, it's amazing how much we think about them. For many people, it's actually the only time we think about them.

And then it tends to fade away. Or not. There are extraordinary resurgences. Individuals you think about for ten years, or a hundred, or a thousand years after their death. Can we deny that this is a sign of presence?

What we would like to know is whether this presence is conscious. Does that dead person know they are here? I daresay they do, but as I am dead, people will say I'm protecting my own interests. Not to mention that I'm not just any old dead person either.

But even then, I don't know. The only dead person I have ever been is myself. Maybe all dead people feel just as present as I do.

What disappears when you die is time. And oddly enough, it takes time to notice this. Music becomes the only thing that allows you to maintain a vague notion of time: were it not for its forward movement, the dead person would no longer grasp what is passing by.

After several chants, I was placed in the sepulcher. A lot of people are in greater fear of being buried than of dying: there's nothing the least bit absurd about such a terror. Dying, why not? But to be shut away in a tomb, possibly with other dead bodies: what a nightmare! Cremation reassures some and frightens others. A justifiable fear. People who shout loud and clear, "Do what you like with my body, I don't care! I'll be dead, it's all the same to me," have obviously not given the matter much thought. Do they really have so little respect for the pound of flesh that enabled them to go through life for so many years?

I have no suggestions regarding the issue; a rite is required, that's all. And fortunately, there's always a rite. In my case, it was performed very quickly, which is normal for a condemned man. An execution followed by a state funeral: not something anyone has ever seen.

I was wrapped gently in a shroud and placed in a recess in the tomb, a sort of bunk. The people left me and closed the door to the sepulcher.

And then I experienced a moment of pure dizziness: I was alone with my death. It could have gone very badly. Is it because I am Jesus that it was so wonderful? I hope not. I would like it to be like this for as many dead people as possible. The moment the dying was finished, my party began. My heart burst, rejoicing. A symphony of jubilation resounded inside me. I went on lying there to explore the joy of it until I couldn't take it anymore. Then I stood up and danced.

The most grandiose music of the present, past, and future poured through my breast and I knew infinity. Usually it takes time to understand the beauty of a piece of music and to let oneself be carried away. But I was able to sense the sublime from the very first time I listened. Not all of this music was human, even if much of it was: it also came from the planets, the elements, and the animals, and other sources that were not obviously identifiable.

There was also a mechanical aspect to my joy: when it comes to our states of mind, the highs tend to follow the lows. But I was touched to realize that this principle of compensation applied even after death.

When the tomb no longer sufficed to contain my exultation, I went out. There has been much debate regarding the degree to which magic helped me. To me, it seemed so natural that I cannot answer. It felt good being outside. The silence that followed the music was a delight I greatly appreciated.

It was windy, and I breathed deeply. Don't ask how a dead man manages to do this. Those who have been amputated retain feeling in their lost limbs, so I imagine that the one can explain the other. I have never stopped feeling the things that were worth it.

I have begun eternal life. This set expression doesn't mean anything to me yet: the word eternity only has meaning for mortals.

There are several versions of the events that followed. Here is my version: by walking around wherever I liked, I happened upon the people I love. What could be more natural? I had no desire to visit places I didn't like, or to go and spend my time with bores.

How do I explain that I was seen and heard? I don't know. It's not a banal occurrence, but it is not unique, either. There have been other cases throughout history of dead people who have been seen and heard, possibly more than that if there is some sort of affinity between the living and dead. There have been famous cases and those that remained unknown. If we had to keep a list of every time someone had a troubling encounter with the dead, we could fill entire telephone directories.

I call on everyone to testify: anyone who has lost loved ones has experienced such inexplicable moments. Some have even had epiphanies with people they didn't know. In truth, there are no limits to what we call living.

This has not prevented—and will not prevent—a sizable proportion of the population from asserting that after death, there is nothing. Such a conviction does not shock me, other than by its peremptory tone and above all by the superior intelligence its proponents pride themselves in possessing. Does this come as any surprise? A sentiment of greater intelligence is always the sign of a deficiency.

I say to you honestly: I am not more intelligent. And I do not even see where the interest of such a claim might lie. Any fantasy of equality I might have is no greater than any fantasy of superiority—futile causes both, for the quality of a human being cannot be measured. Any more than there is a passive or active voice in what is believed to be my final miracle: did I resuscitate or was I resuscitated? If I analyze what went through me, I would say that I was resuscitated. I let it happen to me. The third day? I felt no such thing. When I went from my living state to being dead, I underwent a significant change of perception, particularly where duration is concerned. After I died, was my fate any different from that of mortals? I have no way of knowing, but I have a hunch that I'm not the only one who experienced it as if it were.

A great writer will say that upon dying, the feeling of being in love vanishes and is transformed into universal love. I wanted to verify this by going to see Madeleine. Before she even noticed my presence, I was deeply moved to see her again. The memory of my body took her in my arms, she held me in a furious embrace, none of our passion had changed.

The same writer will explore this topic in his short story entitled "The End of Jealousy". The narrator, jealous to the point of insanity, is cured of his disease at the moment of his death, and simultaneously no longer feels in love. This writer has a very special conception of jealousy: in his eyes, it constitutes the greater part of love.

As I was also once an ordinary man, I recalled that, when I was alive, I found the thought of Madeleine with another man very unpleasant. Now, I have to admit that the prospect leaves me indifferent. And so, the writer was right: jealousy leaves no trace after death. But he was wrong, at least as far as I was concerned: jealousy and being in love do not overlap.

If I appeared so often to those I love, it was more to honor my father's message than out of a deep need. That must be another marked difference from being alive: love no longer engenders such a need for contact. Particularly if the separation did not occur due to a misunderstanding or crisis. I do not doubt Madeleine's love, and I know that she does not doubt mine: why go on meeting so often? What is true for her is all the more so for everyone else.

It's not about coldness. It's about trust. Of course I was moved to see some of my disciples and friends again. And their happiness on seeing me in such good shape was reflected on me. What could be more natural? And yet, while I was living through these festive moments, I was eager for them to end. The increased tension was rather hard to bear. I wanted some peace and quiet. I could sense that my friends wanted a great deal from me, and I tried to respond. It was for them and not for me.

If you reproach your departed loved ones with not appearing before you, do not forget that you are the one who needs them and not the other way around. When we truly love someone, do we require that they sacrifice themselves for us? Isn't allowing those we love a bit of selfish tranquility the finest proof of our devotion? That takes less effort than you might think, merely trust.

In truth, if your departed loved ones remain silent, be glad. It means they have died in the best way. That they are having a good experience of death. Do not infer that they do not love you. They love you in the most wonderful way: by not forcing themselves to go into unpleasant contortions for your sake.

It is a sweet thing to be dead. Coming back to you is rather trying. Just imagine: it's winter, you're lying under your duvet in the coziness of rest and warmth. Even if you cherish your friends, do you feel like going out in the cold to tell them so? And if you are the friend, do you really want to oblige the person you miss to face the discomfort of wintry weather just to reassure you?

If you love your dead, trust them enough to love their silence.

P eople have used the word abnegation when talking about me. Instinctively, I don't like it. My sacrifice was already such a mistake: do I really have to be burdened with the cardinal virtue that leads to it?

I don't see the slightest trace of that disposition in myself. People afflicted with abnegation tend to say, with a pride I find out of place, "Oh, I'm not important, I don't matter."

Either they are lying—and why tell such an absurd lie? Or they are telling the truth, and it is beneath them. To want not to matter is cowardice, misguided humility.

Everyone matters, to such a colossal degree that it is immeasurable. Nothing is more important than the very thing one claims is infinitesimal.

Abnegation implies a disinterested attitude. I am not disinterested, because I am a lever. I aspire to contagion. Dead or alive, everyone has the power to become a lever. There is no greater power.

Hell does not exist. If the damned exist, it is because there will always be killjoys. We have all met at least one of them: the individual who is constantly frustrated, chronically unsatisfied, the one who, when invited to a splendid feast, will see only the fare that hasn't been served. Why should they be deprived of their passion for complaining at the time of their death? They are certainly entitled to make a mess of their own death.

The deceased also have the possibility to meet amongst themselves. I have noticed that they nearly always abstain from it. However intense their friendships or love affairs once were, when they are dead, they no longer have much to say to each other. I don't know why I'm describing this phenomenon in the third person, because, in the end, it applies to me, too.

It's not a matter of indifference, but another way of loving. It all unfolds as if the dead had become readers: their relationship with the universe is like reading. It demands calm, patient attention, and thoughtful decoding. All of this requires solitude—a solitude conducive to a flash of brilliance. In general, the dead are not as stupid as the living.

What is this reading that keeps us so busy once we have died? The book takes shape depending on our desire; our desire gives rise to the text. We are in that luxurious situation where we are both author and reader: writers who create for their own enchantment. No need of pen or keyboard when you are writing in the cloth of your delight.

If we don't seek out encounters, it's because they remind us of our individuality as living beings, something we no longer particularly desire. When he came to find me, Judas called me by my first name, which surprised me.

"Had you forgotten your name is Jesus?"

"Forgotten is not the right word. I'm just not obsessed with it, is all."

"You don't know how lucky you are. I think of little else: I betrayed you. I'm the bad guy in your story."

"If you don't like it, think about something else."

"What else could I think about?"

"Don't you have some pleasurable place to go to in your thoughts?"

"I don't understand your question. I'm the man who betrayed Christ. How do you expect me not to be obsessed by that?"

"If that's what you want, you can stew over it for ever and ever."

"You see! You're encouraging me to feel remorse!"

That's not what I had said. I felt a strange emotion on discovering that misunderstandings could survive beyond death.

What remains of my time as a living person named Jesus?

On their deathbed, the dying often say, "If I could do it all over . . ."—and they specify what they would do all over and what they would change. This proves they are still alive. When you're dead, you feel neither approval nor regret with regard to what you've done or not done. You see your life as a work of art.

At the museum, when you stand before a canvas created by a great master, you never think, "Now if I were Tintoretto, I would have done it like that instead." You gaze at the painting, you take note. And just suppose that you actually were that famous Tintoretto once upon a time, you don't judge yourself, you simply state, "That's me, I can tell from that brushstroke." You don't wonder whether this had anything to do with good and evil, and the thought never even occurs to you that you could have done things differently.

Even Judas. Above all, Judas.

I never think back to the crucifixion. It wasn't me.

I contemplate what I liked, what I do like. My trifecta is still working. Dying is no longer really newsworthy, but it's been worth the detour. Dying is better than death, just as loving is much better than love.

The big difference between my father and me is that he is love, and I am loving. God says that love is for everyone. I who am loving, I see very well that it is impossible to love everyone in the same way. It's a question of breath.

In English, the word is too simple. In Ancient Greek, breathing translates as *pneuma*: an admirable find to express the notion that breathing cannot be taken for granted. English, that eminently practical language, has only preserved, for use in everyday life, words like *pneumatic*.

When you're dealing with someone you suspect you don't like very much, you say that you cannot stomach them. This digestive malaise may then make it difficult to breathe in the presence of that bothersome person.

To use the word breathtaking about someone implies just the opposite: first your breath is taken away from you, then you breathe too much. You feel this hopeless need to breathe in the person whose presence knocks you off your feet.

Even though I'm quite dead, I still feel the dizziness of breath. The illusion is playing its part to perfection.

The one thing I do mourn is thirst. I miss drinking less than the urge that inspires it. A learned synonym for drunkard is dipsomaniac. *Dipsa* is Greek for thirst, but maniac, as far as I'm concerned, is a contradiction in terms, and one I was not in danger of deserving.

To experience thirst, you must be alive. I lived so intensely that I died thirsting.

Perhaps that is what is meant by eternal life.

My father sent me here on earth to spread the faith. Faith in what? In him. Even if he did deign to include me in the concept through the notion of the trinity, I find it mind-boggling.

I came to this conclusion in no time. Moreover, how often did I say to this or that person in distress, "Your faith has saved you"? Would I have lied to these unfortunate people? The truth is that I tried to outsmart my father. I noticed that the word faith had a strange property: it became sublime, provided it was intransitive. The verb "to believe" obeys an identical law.

To believe in God, to believe that God was made man, to have faith in the resurrection: that all sounds a bit shaky. The things we don't like to hear also offend our spirit. It sounds stupid because it is. It all remains pretty lowbrow, like in Pascal's wager: believing in God means placing your bets on him. The philosopher even goes so far as to tell us that no matter the outcome of the raffle, we are sure to win.

And what about me in the middle of all this: do I believe? In the beginning, I agreed to this crazy scheme because I believed in the possibility of changing mankind. Fat lot of good that did. I managed to change maybe three people at the very most. And besides, what an idiotic belief! You really must know nothing about anything to think you can change someone. People change only if it comes from within, and it is extremely rare for them to really want to change. Nine times out of ten, their desire for change is about other people. "This has to change," a phrase you hear *ad nauseam*, always signifies that it's people who ought to change.

Have I changed? Yes, certainly. Not as much as I would have liked. I may be credited for what I really tried to accomplish. I confess I get irritated with people who are constantly telling you they've changed when all they've really ever known is the desire to change.

I have faith. This faith has no object. That doesn't mean I don't believe in anything. Believing is beautiful only in the absolute sense of the term. Faith is an attitude and not a contract. There are no boxes to tick. If we knew the nature of the risk that faith consists of, our impulse would not go beyond calculating probability.

How do we know when we have faith? It's like love, you just know. You don't need to think about it to figure it out. In gospel music they say "And then I saw her face, yes I'm a believer." That's just what it is, and it shows how similar faith and being in love really are: you see a face and suddenly everything changes. You didn't even gaze at that face, you just caught a glimpse of it. That simple epiphany was enough.

I know that for a lot of people, that face will be mine. I've convinced myself that it has no importance whatsoever. And yet, if I want to be perfectly frank, which I do, it leaves me dumbfounded.

You have to accept the mystery: you cannot imagine what other people see in your face.

There is a counterpart that is every bit as mysterious: I look at myself in the mirror. What I see in my face, no one can know. It's called solitude.